TARA LIPINSKI

TRIUMPH ON ICE

D0802123

TARA LIPINSKI

TRIUMPH ON ICE

AN AUTOBIOGRAPHY
as told to Emily Costello

BANTAM BOOKS
NEW YORK · TORONTO · LONDON · SYDNEY · AUCKLAND

TARA LIPINSKI: TRIUMPH ON ICE

A Bantam Book / October 1998

The Starfire logo is a registered trademark of Bantam Books, a division of
Bantam Doubleday Dell Publishing Group, Inc. Registered in U.S. Patent
and Trademark Office and elsewhere.

ISBN: 0-553-57136-2

Published simultaneously in the United States and Canada

Bantam Books are published by Bantam Books, a division of Bantam
Doubleday Dell Publishing Group, Inc. Its trademark, consisting of the
words "Bantam Books" and the portrayal of a rooster, is Registered in
U.S. Patent and Trademark Office and in other countries. Marca Regis-
trada. Bantam Books, 1540 Broadway, New York, New York 10036.

PRINTED IN THE UNITED STATES OF AMERICA

OPM   10   9   8   7   6   5   4   3   2

To my mom:

You have been there for me through good times and bad, and sacrificed so much to support me and my dreams. Without all your pep talks and smiles, that brought me smiles, I know I couldn't have gone this far.

I Love You,
Tara

CONTENTS

CONTENTS

IMPORTANT
EVENTS

1974   My parents, Jack Lipinski and Patricia Brozyniak, wed on May 4 in Bayonne, New Jersey.

1982   I'm born on June 10 in Philadelphia. My parents name me Tara after the plantation in *Gone With the Wind*. (That's Mom's favorite movie.)

1984   I see my first Olympics on TV.

1985   Mom takes me roller skating for the first time. It's almost a disaster! I get upset when she tries to put those ugly brown rental skates on my feet. Sorry, Mom!

1989   My parents take me ice skating for the first time. I'm awful, but only for the first hour. Soon after, I start taking lessons at the University of Delaware.

1991   Dad gets a big promotion. We move to Sugar Land, Texas. Mom and I have to get up at four in the morning so that I can skate. *Yawn!*

1993   Mom and I move to Delaware, where our sleeping habits get back to normal. I begin home tutoring through a private school. Dad stays in Texas with our dogs but visits us as often as possible.

1995   I get a new coach: Richard Callaghan. Mom and I move once more, this time to Bloomfield Hills, Michigan.

1996   I win a bronze medal at the United States Figure Skating Championships. American officials decide I've also earned the right to compete at the Worlds.

My first Worlds as a senior. I finish fifteenth.

At the U.S. Postal Service Challenge in Philadelphia, I become the first woman ever to land a triple loop–triple loop combination in competition.

1997   I skate my best and win the United States Figure Skating Championships in Nashville. With the medal comes a trip to Switzerland to compete in the World Championship.

In Switzerland, I skate two strong programs with no major mistakes. I win the World Championship. At fourteen, I'm the youngest figure skating champion ever!

1998   At the United States Figure Skating Championships, I compete for one of three spots on the U.S. Olympic team. I have a difficult short program and place fourth. But I come back with a solid long program and end up second. Japan, here I come!

At the Olympics in Nagano, I skate a technically and artistically strong short program and long program. Six judges award me first-place ordinals. I am the youngest Winter Olympic gold medalist in history!

TARA LIPINSKI

TRIUMPH ON ICE

Prologue

Four Minutes That Changed My Life

February 20, 1998.

A day I will never forget.

I was skating at the XVIII Winter Olympics in Nagano, Japan. I'd done well during my short program two days earlier, which put me in second place. Michelle Kwan was first, and she had just skated a long program that looked unbeatable.

Everyone expected me to take the silver medal. But my coach told me I could win the gold if I skated my best and held nothing back. I was nervous before getting onto the ice, but I remember telling myself that I didn't want to be disappointed when I finished.

I took my position on the ice. My music began, and I started to skate. My nerves went away, and I felt loose and warmed up. Everything was flowing. I remembered what my coach had said, and I skated with my whole heart. I soared through my

1

jumps and danced through my footwork. I let my excitement show on my face and in the way I moved.

As I skated the final elements in my program, I felt pure joy. I had just given the performance of my life in the most important competition I'd ever entered.

I struck my final pose, but I was only able to hold it for a few seconds. How could I stay still when so much happy energy was moving through my body? I raced across the ice, wishing I knew how to hold on to this moment forever.

When my scores came up, I let out a shout. I'd won! I had just become the youngest Winter Olympic gold medalist in history!

1

EARLY LIFE

I don't come from a skating family.

In fact, my mom and dad don't skate at all.

When I was little, Mom didn't even like watching figure skating. She got annoyed when the Olympics interrupted her TV programs. But *my* interest in the Games developed when I was just two years old, during the 1984 Olympics. This is what Mom says happened:

I was playing in front of the TV while Mom did some chores in the kitchen. The Olympics were on, but I wasn't paying much attention until a group of athletes started to receive their medals. Suddenly I was fascinated. The athletes were standing on podiums, clutching flowers. It looked very exciting.

Back then, my parents kept my toys in Tupperware containers. As soon as the medal ceremony was over, I turned one of the containers upside down. Pretending the container was a podium, I climbed on top.

Mom came out into the living room to see what I was doing.

"I want some flowers and a ribbon," I told her. "So I can be like the people on TV." I didn't ask Mom for a medal because I hadn't even noticed the medals.

Mom found some dried flowers for me to hold. And she tied a ribbon around my neck. That made me happy.

I think that story is amusing when Mom tells it now. I also think that in a way my reaction was an omen—that I was destined to go to the Olympics.

At that time, my family lived in Sewell, New Jersey. If I close my eyes and imagine New Jersey, I remember it always being sunny and warm. Of course, it couldn't have been. New Jersey has dark winters and rainy days just like any other northern state. I think I remember New Jersey being sunny because I was so happy there. My uncle Phil, who's actually my mom's cousin, and my aunt Edith lived just down the street with their sons, Eric and Brian.

Our families were together so much that people used to think we lived in the same house. Uncle Phil, Aunt Edith, Eric, and Brian are all a big part of my New Jersey memories.

I remember the Cabbage Patch Kids doll Uncle Phil gave me when I was really little. Her name was Portia. She was my favorite doll for a long time, even though I used to get in trouble for leaving her out in the rain.

I remember playing miniature golf with Eric. That didn't work out too well. Eric and I both hate to lose.

My dad's mom also lived nearby. I called her Babci. That's short for *Babcia,* which means "grandmother" in Polish. Babci had a big glass cabinet filled with little porcelain figures. I especially loved the porcelain elves, and Babci used to let me play with them. She also let me mess around with her sewing machine.

Those years seemed magical to me, but they must have been hard for my parents. Dad was going to law school while working full-time.

Mom's job was finding ways to keep me busy, and it wasn't easy. Everyone tells me I was a really active baby. I stood up at six months and had started running around by my first birthday. By the time I turned two, I was riding a tiny bicycle my parents had given me. I knew how to crawl out of my crib, and I howled if Mom tried to put me in a playpen. The only way to make me happy was to let me run around until I was tired enough to fall asleep.

That's what Mom had in mind when she first took me roller skating.

2

ROLLING ALONG

One rainy day when I was three, my mother wanted to get me out of the house. She decided to take me to a movie and looked in the newspaper to see what was showing. An advertisement caught her eye. A roller rink just down the street was giving away Care Bears. Mom knew I would like one, and she also figured I'd probably enjoy skating more than sitting still in a stuffy theater. She forgot about the movie. We were off to the roller rink!

Once we got there, Mom paid the entry fee and rented me some skates.

I took one look at the brown rentals and burst into tears. I refused to let Mom put those ugly things on my feet. (I don't actually *remember* doing this. And I feel bad when I hear that I gave my mom such a hard time. But she says three-year-olds can be like that sometimes.) I was raising such a fuss that a woman came over to help. Her name was Ginger Bortz, and she was with a little girl my age.

The little girl was wearing skates, and she was definitely having fun.

"I want to play with her!" I announced.

Mrs. Bortz winked at Mom. "Okay," she told me. "But you can only play with Brittany if you wear skates."

"Okay!" I agreed. I let Brittany's mom put those ugly brown rentals on my feet.

Brittany took my hand, and soon we were circling the rink. The two of us became instant friends. So did our mothers. They had a great time chatting while Brittany and I skated.

The afternoon flew by. When it came time to leave, Mom asked for my complimentary Care Bear. But the man at the rink told her that she hadn't read the advertisement carefully. You only got the Care Bear if you signed up for ten skating lessons. Mrs. Bortz said if Mom signed me up for lessons, she would sign Brittany up, too.

"That way we can all have a day out each week," said Mrs. Bortz.

Mom looked at me. "Do you want to come here every week?"

"Yes!" I said eagerly.

So Mom signed me up for my first ten lessons.

I loved roller skating. I made lots of friends at the rink and enjoyed learning new skills. But the best part of roller skating was performing in front of a crowd.

The rink held a Christmas show, and when we were three and a half, Brittany and I skated to "Grandma Got Run Over by a Reindeer." We were reindeer, along with a bunch of other kids. Our instructor made antlers for our heads.

Then when I was four, Mrs. Bortz suggested that Brittany and I change rinks. That's how I started taking "Tiny Tot" roller skating lessons at a rink in Deptford, New Jersey. After my first class, one of the instructors suggested private lessons.

"Okay," Mom agreed. "One twenty-minute private lesson a week."

So we started going to the rink twice a week—once for my lesson and once for Tiny Tots. The instructors at the rink in Deptford, especially Kathleen DeFelice and Charlie Kirchner, gave me loads of encouragement. And the more I learned, the more I wanted to learn. Before long, Mom was driving me to Deptford *seven* days a week. I did school figures—that's where you trace certain shapes on the floor. I danced pairs. I even speed skated! I liked everything.

Well, there was *one* thing I didn't like: the fact that the rink closed in the evenings while the roller hockey teams played. Mom and I would be on our way home when the boys arrived in their hockey gear, carrying their sticks.

My dance coach, Charlie Kirchner, was also in charge of the hockey league.

"I want a stick too," I told Charlie. And he made me one. Since I was so tiny, Charlie had to cut a regular stick in half. Dad is a big hockey fan, and he proudly decorated the stick with my name.

The next time new hockey teams were forming, I told Charlie I wanted to play.

"Fine," Charlie said.

I was very excited about the idea of joining a team.

The night the teams were picked, the rink was packed with a hundred and fifty boys—and one girl. Me!

My long pigtails weren't the only thing that made me stand out. I was about three years younger than the youngest boys, and the boys took one look at me and told Charlie there was no way they were going to play with a little girl.

Some of their parents agreed. Maybe they thought I would get hurt easily because of my size. Or maybe they thought a girl shouldn't play hockey with boys. It looked as if I wasn't going to be allowed to play, and I felt awful.

But then Charlie told twenty-five of the boys to line up with their backs to him. He asked me to do the same.

"Okay," Charlie called. "I want everyone to skate backward to the wall. One, two, three—go!"

We started to skate. Some of the boys were really struggling. Most of them didn't know how to skate forward, much less backward. I sped right by them and reached the back wall in record time.

"Does anyone have a problem with having Tara Lipinski on their team now?" Charlie asked when the boys finally managed to catch up with me.

No one said a word. Not even the parents.

So I got to play hockey. I was good, too! Because of my size, I could squeeze between the other players and score goals. I loved it—until one day when one of the boys accidentally skated over my fingers.

The pain was enough to convince me to hang up my stick and concentrate on the *glamorous* side of skating.

I had discovered roller skating competitions— and I loved them. I loved the fancy outfits I got to wear. I even loved getting up in the middle of the night so that Mom could drive me to competitions far from home. Part of the fun was staying in my pajamas until we got to our destination.

Back then, competing didn't make me nervous at all. And I won more than fifty plaques, medals, and trophies for roller skating. The most important prize I ever won was the gold medal in the Roller Skating Nationals. I was nine years old and skating in the primary division, which is one level below juvenile. I think I won that competition because I was the only primary skater who could do a heel camel, a roller skating move similar to a camel spin in ice skating. In roller skating, the move is much harder because you have to spin on just your back wheels. My program for that competition also included a five-way combination, or five jumps performed one right after the other.

Long before I hit the Roller Skating Nationals, though, something happened that complicated my life—and brought a lot of fun into it too.

Amanda Nowakowski, one of my nonskating friends, used to come to watch me compete sometimes. Amanda's mother, Janet, was a good friend of my mom's.

Janet watched me roller skating and repeatedly told Mom that I should switch to ice skating. She reminded Mom that roller skating wasn't an Olympic sport, and that the future of a roller skater— even one who won gold medals—was limited.

"I don't care," Mom said. "Tara is having fun. That's all that's important."

"Just *try* it," Janet insisted. "See how Tara does."

Mom told Janet there weren't any decent ice rinks near our house.

But Janet didn't give up.

Finally Mom gave in.

Over Christmas vacation my parents and I set off for a little ice rink nearby. Mom had one thing in mind: proving to Janet that I'd be a *terrible* ice skater.

3

TAKING TO THE ICE

My parents have a photograph of my first time on ice skates. It hangs in the family room of our condo in Detroit. It reminds us all of the day our lives changed forever. I was six years old.

When we arrived at the local ice rink, Dad rented me a pair of skates. Mom helped me lace them up. My parents and I were surprised by how cold it was in the ice rink. We were used to the toasty roller rink. I remember thinking the ice rink even *smelled* different. Kind of like a cross between cold crispness and Zamboni fumes.

I glided out onto the ice—and fell down. I got up. And fell down again. My parents watched me slip all over the ice.

I was a mess. My ankles bent in. My elbows pointed out. And I kept ending up on my backside. My parents were a little surprised I was so awful. After all, I was a natural on roller skates.

But Mom was also relieved. She hadn't *wanted* me to fall in love with ice skating. This small local rink was mostly used for hockey, and the closest rink where I could take ice skating lessons was in Delaware, about an hour away from our house. Getting there meant driving on unfamiliar highways and over several bridges. Not my mother's favorite thing.

Mom and Dad got out the video camera. They taped me falling down. Mom couldn't wait to show her friend Janet how bad I was.

"How about some hot chocolate?" Mom asked after a while.

"Sounds good to me," Dad said.

"No thanks," I said. "I want to keep skating."

So my parents went off to the snack bar and left me on the ice. I kept struggling. I didn't quit because I had already noticed something about ice skating that I liked. My ice skates were *light*. And I knew lighter skates would make doing jumps much easier. That is—if I could figure out how to stay on my feet.

I started to pay attention to what the skaters around me were doing.

When Mom and Dad came back to get me about forty-five minutes later, they were amazed.

I had gotten better. *Much* better. I wasn't falling down anymore, and I had learned how to glide on the ice by watching the other skaters. I had also figured out how to transfer some of my roller skating tricks onto the ice. I was doing axels. And waltz jumps. And I was skating backward.

People were staring and pointing at me. Everyone was surprised I had improved so quickly.

My parents looked at each other.

They both knew that what Mom hadn't wanted to happen *had* happened. I was hooked on ice skating.

"Now try telling Tara you won't drive her to Delaware for lessons," Dad said with a laugh.

Mom groaned. "Impossible."

4

WE MOVE TO TEXAS

The same week that I ice skated for the first time, I started taking lessons at the University of Delaware Ice Skating Science Development Center. That sounds like some sort of government laboratory, but it's just a normal rink.

My coach there was Scott Gregory. He helped me order my very first pair of ice skates and taught me how to lace them up. We worked on transferring all my roller skating moves to the ice. First we tackled my single jumps, and then we quickly moved on to doubles. I also learned how to spin.

Soon I was ready for my first ice skating competition. By chance, it was a regional meet. I skated to Spanish music in a yellow dress Scott had picked out. I took second.

By that time I had fallen in love with ice skating. But my new passion made my life hectic. I'd roller skate on Tuesday, Thursday, and Saturday and ice skate on Monday, Wednesday, and Friday. On Sunday I'd roller skate in the morning and ice skate at night.

As Mom had predicted, our lives weren't made any easier by the fact that the ice rink was an hour away from our house. But before long, Mom mastered the highways and bridges. And I got used to eating dinner off a tray in the back of the car, changing my clothes while zipping over the Delaware Bridge, and doing my homework by a light attached to the dashboard. Usually I'd fall asleep before we got home and Mom would have to carry me to bed.

The summer after I had finished third grade, my dad got a big promotion at work. He became a corporate vice president of the oil refining division of his company. My mother and I were super proud. There was only one problem: Dad's new job was in Houston.

We had to move.

Leaving New Jersey was probably the hardest thing I've ever had to do. I missed my friends, our old house—and especially Uncle Phil and Aunt Edith. And at first I felt out of place in Houston.

Texas just didn't feel like home. It didn't even *look* like home. We moved during the rainy season, and the weather always seemed to be cold and dark. Even now when I think back on that first year, I shudder. It wasn't a happy time.

Then things slowly started to improve. I made friends with a girl across the street whose name is Tara Brooks. It was fun having a friend with the same name. Only she pronounces Tara differently. (She says "TAR-ra.") Tara and I went to the same school and had the same teachers.

Now I really love Texas. I like swimming in our pool. And the mall has all the best stores, including my favorite ice cream parlor, the Marble Slab.

During our first Christmas in Texas, when I was still adjusting to our new surroundings, my parents bought me a horse and a beautiful saddle! It was incredible. Sometimes I pinch myself because I can't believe how generous and nurturing my parents have been. They claim they were just trying to make me feel more like a Texan.

The horse's name was Moonray. He was a big, white, powerful Arabian. Learning how to ride on Moonray was easy. He was a great horse, easy to handle and quick at learning. I got to show him at a local rodeo, where he won a blue ribbon and a silver plate.

But keeping a horse is expensive. You have to pay for food, stables, hay, lessons, tack—we even had to pay a horse dentist to clean Moonray's teeth! Unfortunately, ice skating is also expensive. Especially if you skate as much as I do.

As the bills piled up, my parents realized I had to choose between riding and skating. They gave me two weeks to decide—but the answer was easy. Skating meant everything to me. I wasn't going to give it up for anything. Still, selling Moonray was heartbreaking, and I know that my parents felt bad.

My skating schedule in Texas was hard, too. I had to get up at three in the morning to fit in three forty-five-minute sessions before going off to school. After school, I'd head right back to the rink. The reason I spent so much time on the ice is that I was trying to master my school figures.

School figures are variations on figure eights. At that time, skaters had to learn many different shapes to trace on the ice. When we got to a competition, the officials would choose three for us to skate. Even though I was great at roller skating figures, I was always awful at skating figures on the ice. So I used to spend at least an hour and a half practicing them each day. Then I'd spend another two hours or so working on my free skating. I was very happy when the International Skating Union phased figures out of competition in 1990. Suddenly I had more time to do the fun stuff.

Naturally, I had a new coach in Texas. Megan Faulkner has a really bubbly personality, and we had tons of fun together on the ice—even at the crack of dawn. Megan and I got along so well that she is still one of my coaches.

The summer after we moved to Texas, Mom and I traveled back to Delaware so that I could attend "summer school" at my old rink. While we were there, I started working with a coach named Jeff DiGregorio.

At the end of the summer, Jeff suggested I stay in Delaware and train with him. Mom and I thought about it, but we weren't ready to leave home. We headed back to Texas. Back to Dad, school, Megan, and our four-in-the-morning routine. But by the time that winter drew to a close, it was getting really tough to get up in the middle of the night. Mom and I were constantly tired.

Something had to give. Either I had to give up skating—definitely not an option—or I had to start training during the day. One problem with skating during the day was that it meant giving up school, but my parents and I agreed that a private academy that allows full-time tutoring was worth a try.

A bigger problem was that there wasn't a rink in Houston where I could train during the day.

I wanted to accept Jeff's offer to train in Delaware.

But Dad needed to stay in Texas for his job.

My family had a tough decision to make.

5

BACK EAST AGAIN

My dad stayed in Texas.

Mom and I took an apartment in Delaware.

Our new apartment was only about five minutes from my old rink at the University of Delaware. Life was much easier. Now that I was skating during the day, I was enjoying my time at the rink a lot more. I was awake and ready to attack the challenge of new moves. A tutor taught me in the morning before I skated.

On the weekends, Mom and I drove to Sewell, New Jersey, to spend time with Uncle Phil and Aunt Edith. We traveled the same route we used to drive to the rink. All the old landmarks were still there. We recognized the farmer who had a vegetable stand. And we always stopped for Italian ices at Rosy's Little Farmhouse.

Things were definitely better for me.

But I knew the move was hard on my parents. My skating, which had always been expensive, had just gotten much *more* expensive. Besides paying for ice time and lessons, my parents had to cover rent on the apartment in Delaware, fees for my tutor, and tuition at the private academy in Houston that sent me materials to study. Of course, we also had huge phone bills.

My father had a good job, but his salary couldn't take care of all those extra expenses. Still, my parents knew how important skating was to me. So they decided to refinance our house in Texas and take out a loan. Mom and Dad didn't make a big deal of it, but I knew the extra debt worried them a little.

On top of all that, Mom and I were homesick—this time for Texas!

We missed Dad, even though we talked to him on the phone every day.

We missed Megan. We missed our house, the sunny Texas weather, and our pool.

We also missed our dogs.

My family had three dogs. We got our first one, Camelot, when I was in second grade. He's a bichon frise. For a year we were happy with just one dog, but then Cammy started stripping the wallpaper off our kitchen walls. The vet told us he was lonely. Dad was at work all day. And with all my ice skating and roller skating, Mom and I were hardly ever home. So we decided to get Cammy a friend. We visited several pet stores before we found a bichon puppy that we liked. He was small enough to hold in your hands and absolutely adorable. Perfect for Camelot!

While we were visiting pet shops, my dad spotted a golden retriever puppy. Dad had always wanted a big dog, and he really liked the golden. I fell in love with the puppy too. He was so playful and clumsy.

Dad pleaded and I cried until Mom agreed we should get the retriever too. We named the retriever Brandy and the bichon Lancelot. Camelot was a little surprised when we got home—and definitely not lonely anymore. In fact, things got pretty crazy with two puppies constantly running around and barking.

But that winter all three dogs were back home in Houston, and Mom and I missed them terribly.

That changed on my eleventh birthday. Dad got me a wonderful surprise. It was a wiggling little Yorkshire terrier puppy. He was our new Delaware dog. After a few days, we came up with the perfect name for him: Mischief.

Mischief isn't exactly *bad*. But he does get into things. And he definitely livened up our life in Delaware.

6

MOVING ON UP

In January 1994 Mom, Jeff DiGregorio, and I traveled to Detroit so that I could compete in the Novice Nationals. Megan is from Detroit, so she flew up to meet us. We stayed at the house of a friend of hers for the whole week of competition. Megan also helped us look for a rink where I could train. She asked Richard Callaghan to share some of his ice time at the Detroit Skating Club with us. He agreed.

Megan and I went to the rink. I met Mr. Callaghan and liked him. Mr. Callaghan spent a few minutes watching me skate. He told Megan that what impressed him most was the way I just got on the ice and went to work. I didn't stand gawking at the senior skaters, and I didn't look intimidated. (It was a good thing for me that he liked what he saw, because the following year Mr. Callaghan became my coach. But I'll tell you more about that later.)

When it came time for the competition, the judges liked what they saw too. I finished second.

That summer I was a competition alternate to the Olympic Festival, which was held Fourth of July weekend in St. Louis. Being an alternate meant I would compete if someone else dropped out. As the day of the competition approached, I waited impatiently next to the phone. *Ring,* I thought. And at the last minute, it did!

Someone was dropping out. I could go to St. Louis. I was terribly excited. It was my first really big competition.

The Olympic Festival was like a mini-Olympics. There was an athletes' dormitory, and I got to stay in a room with another competitor. (They don't hold Olympic Festivals anymore, which is a shame because it was a great way to get experience in competing.)

The skating events were held in a large stadium.

People packed the stands. The whole atmosphere was exciting, especially since I was used to small rinks. I loved skating in that arena. And the crowd was so enthusiastic. When I finished, they jumped to their feet and gave me a standing ovation.

I won the gold medal!

And that's not all.

I also set a competition record. At twelve years and three weeks old, I was the youngest gold medalist in Olympic Festival history. Not just in skating—in *any* sport. (Gymnast Shannon Miller had held the record before me. She won when she was twelve years and four months old.)

That's *still* not all. I also won the Mary Lou Retton Award. There was a cash prize, and I got to meet Mary Lou.

I also made the Junior World team. I felt as if a whole new world were opening up to me.

I took the test to qualify as a junior skater late that summer, and passed with flying colors. I could hardly wait for the Worlds!

Between the test and the Worlds, I squeezed in my first-ever international competition. It was called Pokal der Blauen Schwerter, which is German for the Blue Swords Cup. The competition was held in Chemnitz, Germany, in October 1994.

Blue Swords remains one of my all-time favorite competitions because I met so many great people there. My roommate was Erin Elbe, who is now a senior pairs skater. She has become one of my best friends.

And I came in first! That made me look forward to the Worlds even more.

The 1994 Junior World Championship was held over Thanksgiving weekend in Budapest. The city is full of little shops and grand old buildings. Spending the holiday there was a lot of fun. The only thing I missed was a traditional Thanksgiving dinner; turkey is just not a Hungarian specialty.

Since the competition was my first Worlds, I didn't expect to do well. I was really pleased when I finished fourth.

The 1995 United States Figure Skating Championships, which were held the following February, were my first Nationals as a junior. I knew I would be competing with lots of good skaters who had been juniors for a while, so I set the modest goal of finishing in the top five.

About two weeks before the competition, I learned my triple flip jump, and I focused on landing it during my long program. And I did! It was rewarding to see that all the work I'd put into learning a more difficult jump had paid off. I was really pleased when I took second.

After the Nationals Jeff decided it was time for me to move up to the senior division, even though I had only been a junior for a year. A judge from the United States Figure Skating Association came to the rink to watch me skate. He agreed I could become a senior. Not bad for a twelve-year-old!

That spring I traveled to Germany for the Obersdorf Grand Prix Competition. I skated two solid programs and was happy to finish fourth.

The next big event on my skating schedule was that fall, when I competed in the World Junior Selection Competition in Colorado Springs. Now, you may be wondering how I was able to compete for a spot on the *Junior* World team when I'd already moved up to the *senior* division. Trust me—it was perfectly legal.

The United States Figure Skating Association and the International Skating Union have different definitions of *junior* and *senior*. In USFSA-sponsored events, your division is based on skill. In ISU-sponsored events—like the Junior Worlds—a skater's division is based on age. So, for about a year, I competed as a senior in national competitions and as a junior in international ones.

The important thing to know is that I placed second in Colorado Springs, which meant that I got to go to Junior Worlds.

But I still had to qualify for the following year's Nationals. A few weeks later, I took first in a regional meet, the first step in the qualifying process. And since I had already qualified for Worlds, I received a bye for sectionals. (In other words, I automatically advanced through the sectional round without competing.) I was now qualified to go to the following year's Nationals in San Jose and compete in the senior division. Whew!

The Junior Worlds that year were in Australia.

I skated well but only ended up in fifth place. Still, the competition was a blast! Erin Elbe was there. We spent two fun-filled weeks shopping, petting koala bears, and hanging out at a couple of incredible beaches. I'd go back to Australia any day.

7

STARTING AT
MR. CALLAGHAN'S

Two years after moving to Delaware, Mom and I started looking for a new training facility. The University of Delaware is a popular rink, and the freestyle sessions were becoming crowded. I often had to skate during the pairs sessions, which made it difficult for me to train. And Mom and I thought a new coach would be good for me. We traveled all over the country, visiting coaches in Ohio, Colorado, and Connecticut.

Mom and I decided not to visit any coach who was already training an elite female skater. We crossed Frank Carroll off our list because he trains Michelle Kwan. And we didn't consider Mr. Callaghan because he was working with Nicole Bobek, who was that year's U.S. Ladies Singles Champion. (He was also training Todd Eldredge.)

The week before Christmas, Mom and I wound up our tour of training facilities and flew back to Texas. We went to the rink so that Megan could give me a lesson. But before we got inside, Megan came running out to meet us. "You have to go to Michigan!" she said. "Richard Callaghan has an opening."

Megan explained that Nicole Bobek and Mr. Callaghan had decided to go their separate ways.

Mom groaned. "I've met enough coaches," she said. "And we just got back."

But Mom's a trouper. My plea of "Let's try one more, then we'll make a decision" got us back to the airport, and we flew to Detroit. Mr. Callaghan and I worked together for a couple of days. We seemed to click right away. I felt comfortable with him. Although he is strict, I thought he would push me when I got bored or tired. Plus, the Detroit Skating Club was incredibly nice.

After spending Christmas in Texas, I told Mom

and Dad I wanted to train with Mr. Callaghan. My parents agreed it was the best decision. We had finally found my new coach.

Two days later Mom and I were back in Detroit. There was no time to lose. My first Nationals as a senior were only a few weeks away.

In those weeks leading up to the Nationals, I quickly realized that Mr. Callaghan is a great coach. He really understands each element that goes into a winning program: technical, artistic, and mental.

I also found out that I was right when I guessed Mr. Callaghan would be strict. But the discipline he requires has helped me to establish clear goals and to work hard toward achieving them. Mr. Callaghan wants me to succeed. So do I.

While I prepared for the Nationals, Mom and I also got settled. We rented a very nice condo not too far from the Detroit Skating Club, and we put a lot of hours into making it feel like home.

I decorated my room: On a large wall mirror, I taped up photographs of me with Erin Elbe and with my other best friend, senior singles skater Erin Sutton. And I hung a poster titled "Skater's Dream" over my bed. It shows a young girl sound asleep, holding her skates. She's dreaming about the famous skaters Peter and Kitty Carruthers, Jill Trenary, Katarina Witt, and Kurt Browning.

When *I* went to sleep under that poster, I dreamed of the Nationals. And they weren't all happy dreams. Even though I had an excellent new coach, changing coaches right before a big competition is *not* usually a good idea. I was certain the Nationals were going to be a disaster.

Most skaters *are* nervous about the Nationals. The Nationals are where you test yourself against the very best skaters in the country, where you see how your technical ability, artistic expression, and mental resolve stand up under the stress of competition. They're where you prove yourself. With all the recent changes in my life, I was a bundle of nerves.

Mr. Callaghan knew this and was supportive. He didn't try to change anything about the program I'd been skating that season. He just wanted me to do the best I could.

The competition was in San Jose, California. I was the youngest senior-division competitor there. I was so rushed going into the competition, I didn't even have time to set a real goal. *Just skate well,* I told myself. Then I tried to relax and enjoy the thrill of competing against girls I had been reading about in *Skating* magazine: Nicole Bobek, Michelle Kwan, Tonia Kwiatkowski, and others.

I skated my short program, and I came in fifth. What a relief! I had reached my goal of skating well. I felt as if I had gotten over a huge hurdle. *I can do this!* I told myself.

Nicole Bobek was third after the short program. But she was injured and decided to withdraw before the long program. I skated well again and moved up into third place. Tonia Kwiatkowski was second. Michelle Kwan was first.

Usually the three skaters who place at the Nationals go on to the Worlds. But an injured skater has the right to appeal for a spot. The officials had a decision to make. Should they send Nicole or me to the Worlds?

When the officials came to tell me *I* had been chosen, I couldn't believe it. I had been expecting the worst during the entire competition, and now I was going to the Worlds.

By the time we returned to Detroit, I knew our

decision to move there had been the right one. I knew that with Mr. Callaghan as my coach, I'd realize my dream of becoming a top skater.

Only one thing made me sad. Our "Delaware" dog, Mischief, hadn't moved with us. He had gotten too big to travel easily on airplanes. And he seemed to love Texas, where he could play with Camelot, Lancelot, and Brandy. So Mom and I left Mischief in Texas.

There was only one solution: another dog! This time we got a fluffy white Maltese. My friend Erin Sutton got a puppy from the same litter. I named my puppy Coco. Erin named hers Chanel.

Coco is really funny. She plays with a white wool duster that's almost as big as she is. Sometimes it's hard to tell where Coco ends and the duster begins.

8

THE EDMONTON WORLDS

All the senior women skaters in the United States are incredibly talented. Most are capable of doing the same jumps and spins. Mr. Callaghan believes that the skater with the right mind-set—the one who can shut out all the pressure that comes with a competition, and who just gets out on the ice and does her job—is the one who wins.

One competition where my mind-set slipped was the Worlds in 1996. I'd narrowly earned the right to compete there when Nicole Bobek withdrew from the Nationals because of an injury.

The competition was in Edmonton, Alberta, Canada.

Things started well. I placed second, right after

the Japanese skater Midori Ito, in our qualifying group. But things changed for the worse during my short program.

Midori Ito skated right before me. I've always looked up to Midori. She was one of the first women to land a triple axel, and that just amazed me.

While I watched Midori skate, I started thinking about how strange it was that I was competing against skaters from all over the world—skaters I was used to watching on television. The thought kind of freaked me out.

Midori didn't skate that well. As I was getting ready for my turn, I listened to the announcement of her marks. They were low. That made me have a truly bizarre thought: I could *beat* these skaters I had been watching on television. I could beat Midori Ito.

The thought stayed with me as I got onto the ice. I was totally distracted. I was thinking about winning, not about doing my work. My combinations felt totally weird. The timing was all off. I landed my first difficult jump, a triple Lutz. But on my double loop, I fell.

I was stunned. I had just fallen at the Worlds!

How incredibly stupid, I thought as I went into my triple flip—and I missed that too. My dream come true was turning into a nightmare!

My short program didn't feel short. It felt endless. Finally I finished and got off the ice.

Mr. Callaghan was waiting for me. "That's okay," he told me. "It happens. Don't worry, I'm sure you'll do better tomorrow."

I hardly heard his kind words—my scores were coming up, and they were as awful as I'd known they would be. I ended up twenty-third out of thirty.

What a disaster!

Everyone tried to cheer me up: Mr. Callaghan, my new rinkmate Todd Eldredge, Mom, Dad, even the television commentators. I tried to keep my composure and told everyone I was fine. But it wasn't true. I was mad at myself. I had wasted an opportunity.

The next morning I was still upset. I decided the only way to make up for my poor performance in the short program was to skate well in my long program. I wanted to show everyone—including myself—that I deserved to be on the World team. I wanted everyone to know that I could keep up with Midori and all the other skaters.

Mr. Callaghan and I had a talk. He helped me realize that watching Midori skate had been a mistake. Seeing her program had made me focus on scores and winning. I had been thinking about *her* skating when I should have been concentrating on *mine*.

Before my long program, we tried an experiment. I made a point of not watching the other skaters perform. Instead, I sat quietly and thought about what I had to do.

The experiment worked! When I started to skate my long program, my head was in the right place. I entered the first of my triple jumps knowing I'd land it *and* the six triple jumps that followed—including my triple salchow–triple loop combination.

I did.

At the end of my long program, the crowd gave me a standing ovation. The judges placed me eleventh in the free skate. I finished fifteenth overall. I was happy. In a way, coming up from behind was more satisfying than doing well all along. I felt as if I was going out with a bang.

Todd Eldredge won the men's title with two sparkling programs. I was so impressed. I couldn't believe that we actually had the same coach. I felt as if I'd hit the big time!

9

ARTISTIC EXPRESSION

After the Worlds, Mr. Callaghan and I set to work.

We had already changed something important about the way I competed. Now we started tinkering with the way I practiced.

I had a bad habit back then. Whenever I missed a jump in practice, I made myself do it several times in a row. I thought doing the jump over and over would bring me luck and that it was the best way to improve. Mr. Callaghan didn't agree. He explained that doing so many jumps every day put my bones and muscles under enormous stress. Not a good thing. Mr. Callaghan also said I had to stop thinking I'd succeed only if things happened a certain way. He told me I had to adapt to different situations and experiences and still win.

So I quit trying to land all those jumps. It wasn't difficult. I had plenty of other stuff to keep me busy because it was time to create my first programs with Mr. Callaghan.

Unlike most sports, skating is scored by judges. You get two marks. The technical mark reflects the difficulty of the program and how well it's executed. The artistic mark is for the choreography, the musical interpretation, and the flow and balance of the program. For the artistic mark, the judges also consider how well you use the ice and how fast and confidently you skate. The second mark is actually slightly more important, because artistic marks are used to break some ties.

Mr. Callaghan thought I could improve my artistic marks if we created a more sophisticated style for me. But we had to be careful not to go too far. Our goal was to keep the freshness that I had as a fourteen-year-old, but to add a touch of sophistication. To achieve this, we considered everything—my hairstyle, my makeup, my dresses, my music, and my choreography.

The last—choreography—led me to Sandra Bezic. Sandra is a former Canadian pairs champion and probably the most famous skating choreographer ever. She puts together show pieces for the touring ice show *Stars on Ice*. Plus, she's worked with many great skaters. For the 1994 Olympics alone, she choreographed programs for Brian Boitano, Kurt Browning, Josée Chouinard, and Katarina Witt. Sandra is definitely a class act, as Mr. Callaghan would say.

Mom and I met with Sandra in Toronto, where she lives. I liked her right away. She's friendly, pretty, and really gets to know the personality of the skater she's choreographing for.

Sandra believes that the most important part of the choreography is the music and the basic idea that springs from it. In my old long program, I had skated to the sound track from the movie *Speed*. I loved that music because it was so powerful. But this time we wanted a piece of music that said "sophisticated."

We spent three whole days just listening to music. Finding music that sounded good wasn't enough. The music also had to emphasize my technical moves and have some slow parts in it so that I could catch my breath. I also had to react to it emotionally, so that I would look involved with the music as I skated, something the judges reward with high marks.

All year I had heard music that I thought I'd like to skate to. But now that it was time to choose, I couldn't remember any of the scores. Sandra suggested the music from *The Nutcracker*. But I felt as if I had heard it too many times.

After three days we were beginning to think we'd never find anything we liked. Then we finally listened to the sound track from *Sense and Sensibility*.

"This is it!" Sandra and I both said.

What a relief!

For the next week Sandra and I worked on the choreography in an empty rink. Sandra would come up with ideas, and then I'd try them out. We'd keep some sections she created and throw out others. Slowly we built up a new program.

Then Sandra helped me interpret the music. She helped me explore the full range of emotions.

Once we got back to Detroit, Mr. Callaghan

choreographed my short program to the sound track from *Little Women*. The short program is more technical. The International Skating Union even gives us a list of elements we have to include. As a senior, I have to do a double axel, a flying spin, a spiral step sequence, and five other elements.

Along with my new programs came new dresses. Even these were more sophisticated. Jeff Billings made me a beautiful dress for my short program. It was very simple and elegant. Then Mr. Callaghan and I talked to the designer Lauren Sheehan about the kind of dress we imagined for my long program. I got to help pick out colors. My main comment was: No orange! We finally decided on an off-white dress.

The dress Lauren made was definitely a new look for me. Even the cut of the skirt was different from what I normally wore. I thought the dress was perfect the moment Lauren finished sewing it together. Everyone else kept saying, "We need beads!"

Beads? Not for me. Not usually, at least. I am not a glitter queen! I like my dresses plain. But then again, I was trying for a more sophisticated look. I agreed reluctantly to try the beads. And I'm glad I did.

Lauren did a terrific job. You don't notice the beads as much as the way the dress sparkles!

I worked on building my sophistication in another way too. I started working with a ballet instructor, Marina Sheffer.

Marina looks—well, just the way you'd expect a ballet teacher to look. She's tall, with very good posture and long brown hair. And she has a Russian accent. When I first met her, I expected her to be really strict. But she's not.

Mr. Callaghan calls what Marina teaches me applied ballet. That means I don't have to go to a studio and do hours of pliés. I'm happy about that, since I did plenty of pliés when I was taking ballet lessons, from the time I was three to the time I was eleven. Ballet is nice, but I find skating a lot more dynamic.

Marina gives me my lessons at the rink. And no, she doesn't wear a leotard and slippers on the ice. She bundles up in sweats, a coat, and sneakers. Then she stands by the boards and watches my routine. Usually

I do my programs both up close and far away, so that Marina can see me skate as the television cameras will see me and as the judges will see me.

Even though Marina isn't a skater, she knows what's important in skating. She tells me how to move my arms, legs, and neck so that I look more graceful. Working with her on the parts of the program between the jumps and spins has made me a more expressive skater.

Mr. Callaghan and I also set about improving my technical abilities. One of our main goals was helping me cover the ice faster. Skating with more speed could improve my artistic marks by making me look more confident on the ice. To skate faster, I needed stronger leg muscles. But Mr. Callaghan doesn't believe in weight training. He thinks it's better for me to build up my legs by skating regularly, even though it may take a little longer to get results.

Another area we started working on was improving the technique on my double axel, and we worked on improving the overall speed and flow of all my jumps.

Like I said before: We were busy!

10

MY SECOND HOME

After we finished hammering out my programs, Mr. Callaghan and I established a training routine. That routine became a comforting habit. Mr. Callaghan says consistency is important for an athlete, and that regular training keeps you in good shape, so that when it comes time to compete, you're ready. I agree.

That was one of the reasons I didn't mind training six days a week. The other reason was that being at the Detroit Skating Club was fun.

This is what my average skating day was like during my first winter at Mr. Callaghan's:

My alarm went off about seven-fifteen.

I'd ignore it until my mom shouted, "Shut off the alarm!" I'd shut it off, then fall back to sleep. If

I was lucky, I'd wake up by seven-forty-five. If I slept any later than that, I was seriously late!

After my room was straightened up, I'd go downstairs for breakfast. I'd usually have a bagel. Sometimes eggs, too. Mom and I would feed the dog and pack a lunch to take to the rink.

Then I'd stretch in front of the television while I watched *Good Morning, America* or *Today*. When my muscles were good and limber, I'd dash upstairs to get dressed.

Usually I'd wear a skating dress or leotard with a sweater over it. My hair went up in a ponytail or bun. I'd also bring gloves to the rink. They protected my hands when I fell. (Some people think good skaters never fall. That's not true at all! We fall a lot. But it doesn't usually hurt because we know how to fall safely.)

I'd wear running shoes to the rink and carry my skates. I get two new pairs of skates every year. One pair I skate in all the time. The other pair is my "in case" pair—I keep them just in case my regular skates get lost or worn out.

I'd *hate* to lose a pair of nice broken-in skates. New skates are the worst! Even though I get them custom made (a must for a serious skater), they're still always really stiff. If they were too soft, they wouldn't give me enough support out on the ice. So even though the skates are made specially for my feet, breaking them in takes about three weeks—and the first week is *awful.* I get blisters all over my feet.

But once the skates are broken in, they're really comfortable. So I take good care of them to make sure they last. That means wearing my skate guards until just before I get on the ice. Still, every spring my skates start to break down and I have to get a new pair.

Anyway, as soon as I'd collected my skates and the rest of my gear, Mom would drive me to the rink. Our condo was near the Detroit Skating Club, so it was a fast ride. I liked to get to the rink around eight-thirty. That gave me plenty of time to jump around and warm up before my ice time began.

Several other skaters shared the ice with me: Todd, the Polish national champion Zuzanna Szwed, Erin Sutton, and Erin Pearl. We all pretty much did our own thing, but it was nice to have company. The rink had a totally different atmosphere than when you go for an open skate at a public rink. The mood was quiet and serious. Still, it wasn't *that* quiet because we skated to music, and sometimes we turned it up pretty loud.

By nine-thirty I'd have been skating for a while and my muscles would be loose and warm. I'd be ready for my first lesson of the day. Mr. Callaghan came onto the ice to help me train for my long program. I usually ran through the whole program once. Then Mr. Callaghan would tell me where I needed work. He wasn't really into ordering me around or forcing me to do things. He just told me what he thought I needed to do to succeed. And of course I followed his advice.

At ten-thirty I usually took a break for about fifteen minutes. I'd have something to drink—skating is sweaty work—and visit the bathroom.

Then I'd hit the ice for another forty-five-minute session. Mr. Callaghan and I usually met again during this period. This time I trained for my short program.

At eleven-thirty I would get an hour's break for lunch. I almost always ate with Erin Sutton.

My lunch was usually something like turkey,

yogurt, a chocolate chip cookie, and chocolate milk. Most athletes have to be very careful not to gain weight. But I could actually use a few more pounds! So I made sure that what I ate was healthful, without worrying about whether it was fattening.

After we were done eating, Erin Sutton and I often played Foosball against Erin Pearl and another skater. Erin Sutton and I are both pretty terrible at Foosball, but we had a good time playing together.

At twelve-forty-five I would be back on the ice. This time Mr. Callaghan would work with me on specific elements—jumps, spins, or moves I was just learning. Later in the afternoon, we'd run through my long program one more time.

My mother stayed at the rink with me all day. She always watched my lessons with Mr. Callaghan from her seat in the bleachers. Sometimes she brought a magazine or book with her, but I liked her to watch me skate so that later we could discuss what happened.

A few times a week, I worked with Craig Maurizi, an assistant coach. He was a lot of fun to work with, and he made me laugh a lot.

I also spent about half an hour each afternoon with Marina Sheffer, my ballet instructor.

The rest of the time, about half of my total training hours, I skated on my own. Sometimes I asked Todd for help. If I was having trouble with a jump, he'd watch and tell me what I was doing wrong. Maybe one of my arms was too low. Or maybe I didn't have enough speed.

Todd gave me advice about a lot more than just jumps. He told me how to keep from getting too nervous before a competition. *He* never seemed nervous, although he said he was.

After I moved to Detroit, Todd became like a big brother to me. Sometimes he was sweet and thoughtful—like when he gave me a few words of encouragement before a big meet. And sometimes he was a big pain! He teased me all the time. One of his favorite tricks was hiding my skate guards, and he loved to tickle me.

Todd also made fun of me for being such a perfectionist. For example, say he noticed me making a face as I came out of a combination.

"That looked good," he'd say as he skated by.

"It was awful!" I'd call after him.

I'd try the combination again. This time I'd be happy with it and I'd land with a big smile on my face.

"That was awful," Todd would say. "You'd better do five more!"

Sometimes Todd's teasing made me really mad. But not often. I really valued our friendship.

It's funny to think about it now, but when I first got to Detroit, Todd intimidated me. I was a little in awe of him, especially after he won at the Worlds. So it's extra nice that we're friends now.

I finished up at the rink by two-thirty or three o'clock. Then Mom and I headed home so that I could go to school.

Actually, it was more as if school came to me. One of the upstairs rooms in our condo was fixed up like a classroom. It had a small blackboard, a desk, books, a microscope, and a computer.

Tutors came in to teach me all the same subjects the students back at my school in Texas were studying.

Some people think home tutoring is a breeze, but it's actually pretty intense. When you're one-on-one with a tutor, you can't goof around or doze off. Also, the lesson is tailored to me. My tutors move quickly through the things I understand and spend lots of time on stuff I find confusing.

Math and science are my favorite subjects. Literature is my *least* favorite, which is strange because I really like some books. But dusty old tomes like *Wuthering Heights* are just not my style.

Every time my tutors come, they sign a sheet and write down how many hours they spend with me. That sheet and my grades get sent back to my school in Houston. I get good grades, mostly As and a few Bs. The school also tells my tutors what material we have to cover. Sometimes it's hard to concentrate on studying when so many exciting things are happening. But when I start to lose my focus, my mom reminds me that someday it will be time for me to hang up my skates and start a new life. She wants to make sure I can get into a good college. And that means making good grades.

I keep changing my mind about what I want to do for a career. Lately I've been thinking about becoming a lawyer. My dad went to law school when I was little, and I loved hearing about all the different cases he was studying. I especially like the thought of being a plaintiff's attorney, because I like helping others and that's the lawyer who represents the people's side.

After I finished with my tutors, I'd do a little homework. Then I came downstairs and watched *Wheel of Fortune.* I loved solving the puzzles, especially the bonus round at the end. I usually watched *Jeopardy!* too, but it was harder.

Mom and I ate dinner during this time. We cooked steak and vegetables or pasta. One of my favorite things is pasta with a simple tomato sauce. I also like salad. And for dessert, nothing beats Oreo-cookie brownies.

After dinner I'd do more homework and take time out for favorite TV shows like *Party of Five* and *Friends.*

I tried to go to bed by ten so that I could get up and start again in the morning.

On Sunday morning I'd usually go to church with my mom. If I was in Houston or Dad was in Detroit, the three of us went together. In Detroit we went to St. Hugo's, a Roman Catholic church not too far from our condo. In Houston we went to St. Laurence's. I love the warm, welcoming feeling I get from attending Mass. Church helps me feel grounded—even when I'm constantly jetting off to competitions and appearances.

After we got home from church, I'd sometimes do some sewing. I got interested in sewing back when I was a little kid. My grandma had a sewing machine that she used to let me play with. Now I have a machine of my own. I made a stuffed rabbit, which wasn't easy. I also made some throw pillows. The pillows are made of material that's printed with—you guessed it!—ice skaters. I sewed lace all around the edges. Maybe someday I'll get good enough to make my own clothes or my own skating costumes. Then again . . . maybe not!

I spent most of my free time in Detriot hanging out with Erin Sutton. Erin slept over at my house all the time. We rented movies, played Ping-Pong in my basement, or just listened to music.

We also spent lots of time at the mall, where we shopped for clothes and shoes. And we were always looking for new stuffed frogs to buy. That's right,

Erin and I share a strange hobby: collecting frogs! We started when we discovered that we had matching frog rings.

Now we each have a huge frog collection. I have about forty. Mom bought me a special rack where I store them all. I even have a frog on ice skates.

Another one of my favorite activities is talking to Erin Elbe on the phone. I hate the fact that one of my best friends lives hundreds of miles away in California. But Erin Elbe and I visit each other as frequently as possible. Between visits, marathon sessions on the phone help us stay up to date on each other's lives.

I also like to hang out at home with my parents. During those years in Detroit, Mom and I got to see Dad only about once every two weeks, but we made the most of the time we had together. My family is small, but it's also super close. I think my parents are incredible for having supported and encouraged my skating all these years. I couldn't have accomplished so much without them.

11

COMPETING

I've been in so many competitions over the years that I've lost count. Still, each competition is exciting, and competing is definitely what I like best about skating. I love getting a break from training, traveling to a new place, staying in hotels, and performing for a crowd. Another great part about competitions is seeing my skating friends, particularly Erin Elbe.

But there is one thing I don't much like about competing: flying in airplanes. I'm scared of heights. As long as the plane is big, I'm not too jittery. But the little ones totally terrify me.

Once, Todd and I were invited to do a show in Mobile, Alabama. We were supposed to fly down on a Learjet. I'd never been in a Learjet before, and I thought it sounded big.

Todd teased me about it. He said Learjets took off like the space shuttle, straight up into the air! I didn't believe him. But his teasing did make me a little nervous. Although not as nervous as I felt when I actually saw the plane. It was tiny! So tiny, I couldn't make myself board. I had to miss the show.

Mom usually helps me relax during flights. She and Mr. Callaghan always accompany me to competitions and events. Once we arrive, I try to practice twice a day, and Mr. Callaghan corrects any minor problems he sees.

Sometimes on television you see coaches hovering over their athletes, whispering in their ears, telling them what to do. Mr. Callaghan isn't like that. He's very supportive, but he doesn't baby me. He believes it's important for me to be independent—to walk into a competition feeling confident and do my work, all on my own. Usually I do feel confident. Knowing that my coach doesn't think I need a lot of attention helps.

Of course, Mr. Callaghan and my parents are there if I truly need them. And they never forget to cheer me on!

When I go to a new city to compete or to perform in an exhibition, I try to do some cheering too. Cheering up, that is. I like to visit kids in a local hospital. The first time I visited a hospital was in Long Beach, California. I was doing a televised exhibition. The sponsor of the show was making a donation to the City of Hope, a hospital and research center for kids with cancer and other serious illnesses. The sponsor had promised that one of the skaters would visit the hospital.

I volunteered, and then I started to get nervous. I wasn't sure how I would react to seeing a bunch of kids who were ill.

But once we got to the hospital, everything was fine. We went from room to room, visiting the young patients. Most of them weren't big skating fans, so we talked about the sports they liked. Brightening up their day made me feel good. The kids paid me back by smiling or giving me a hug or just saying thanks.

Each time I visit a children's hospital I get a reality check. I realize that missing a jump or having a bad practice isn't the end of the world. I'm reminded of how lucky I've been.

12

THREE BIG MEETS

Less than a year after the Edmonton Worlds, I competed in the International Skating Union's fall championship series.

The series has six competitions leading up to the final. Each skater is assigned two of those competitions by the United States Figure Skating Association. You get a set number of points for a first-place finish, fewer for second place, fewer still for third, and so on. At the end, the six competitors with the most points meet up for the championship final.

I was assigned Skate Canada and the Trophée Lalique.

Skate Canada, which was held in Kitchener, Ontario, was the first competition of the year for me. It was a great way to begin. I performed my new short program. The audience liked it and applauded loudly. The judges liked it and placed me third.

Then it came time to try out my new long program, which was much more difficult than the one I had performed the year before. I landed three clean combinations, including my triple salchow–triple loop.

I finished second overall. And I got my first international medal as a senior skater!

A few days later I was on a plane to Paris to compete in the Trophée Lalique. That competition was a lot of fun because it was my first trip to Paris. I got to see the Eiffel Tower and the Cathedral of Notre Dame.

I skated well in the short program. But something strange happened during my long program. I got distracted—and lost my place coming out of a spin. I glanced around the rink for a familiar landmark, but I couldn't find one. I panicked and skated in the wrong direction.

Mr. Callaghan smiled and shook his head as I came off the ice. "What happened?" he asked.

"I don't know!" I said. "I got lost."

He reminded me that I would have to do my program in many different arenas. "This is a learning experience, and you'll probably never do that again," he said.

I agreed, and though the final part of my program hadn't gone as planned, I still managed to take home the bronze.

While we were in Paris, we were contacted by the United States Figure Skating Association. One of the American skaters had dropped out of the Nations Cup just days before it was scheduled to begin in Gelsenkirchen, Germany. The U.S. team needed another woman. I agreed to go in the skater's place, even though I wouldn't receive any points for competing.

The Nations Cup competition turned out to be a learning experience too. This time I learned that three competitions in three weeks is too many. I was exhausted, but I skated well and took second. Actually, I came really close to winning. Three judges placed me ahead of Irina Slutskaya of Russia, who won first place with the votes of four judges. Since Irina was ranked third in the world at that point, I was very happy.

I loved playing with the toy bears in my mom's collection (1982).

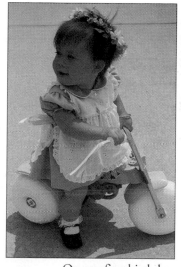

On my first birthday, Grandpa Lipinski gave me a great bicycle. Grandma Lipinski made the pretty dress I wore, and my mom made the wreath. (I sew well too.)

I was always on the go as a kid (1983).

Halloween is great! I love getting into costume! Grandma Lipinski made the mouse outfit I wore when I was two years old.

Walt Disney World is my favorite vacation place. I've been going there every year since I was three years old. That's when I first met Tammy Guitterez, who plays Snow White. She and I have become special friends (1988).

I was a little wobbly the first time I put on figure skates and stepped onto the ice, at age six and a half. But by the time I got off, I knew figure skating was for me. I was hooked.

My cousin Colleen Brozyniak and I always had fun when we got together as kids. Here we're in our Easter best (1987).

My mom, Pat, and I loved hanging out on the beach at the Jersey shore (1988).

The tooth fairy brought me some money when I lost my first baby tooth in 1990.

I started roller skating at age three, and when I was eight I won a silver medal at the National Roller Skating Competition in Texas (above). The next year, I won the gold!

Moonray is the white Arabian horse my parents bought me in Texas. He loved eating carrots (1992)!

In 1995 I had a blast goofing around during time off from the Too Hot to Skate exhibition in Santa Cruz, California.

I'm very close to my uncle Phil. He gave me a skate boot necklace charm that says "Thumbs Up." I wear it all the time. That's my dog Coco (1996)!

Two of my best friends are ice-skaters. Here I am (above) with Erin Sutton (senior singles) at Walt Disney World in 1996. And (at right) with Erin Elbe (senior pairs) at the Sweetwater Country Club in Houston, also in 1996. It's cool that they have the same first name!

I'm crazy about frogs! As you can see, my collection is big—and growing (1997).

A family portrait (1997): my mom, Pat; my dad, Jack; my adorable dog Coco; and me!

Layback spins allow a skater to display her grace (1997 U.S.
Nationals).

My coach, Richard Callaghan, always helps me to focus before I start my program (1997 U.S. Nationals).

© Dave Black 1997

Jumping is my favorite part of figure skating. Each jump happens really quickly, but I never get dizzy (1997 U.S. Nationals).

Duomo/Paul J. Sutton

Judges like to see a high extension during a spiral sequence. I'm improving mine all the time (1997 U.S. Nationals).

Todd Eldredge and I were thrilled to be the 1997 U.S. National Champions. We couldn't have done it without our fabulous coach, Richard Callaghan.

© Paul Harvath 1997

I love competing. I get a real adrenaline rush skating in front of a crowd—and in front of the judges (1997 U.S. Nationals Exhibition).

The crowd was very supportive during every one of my performances (short program at the 1998 Olympics).

It felt great to skate at the Olympics; I didn't hold anything back (1998).

© Dave Black 1998

© Jamie Squire / AllSport 1998

Seeing my scores come up and realizing I'd won the Olympic gold medal was a dream come true! My coach, Richard Callaghan, was ecstatic too (1998).

13

TRIPLE LOOP–TRIPLE LOOP

In late 1996 I signed up to compete at the U.S. Postal Service Challenge in Philadelphia.

About two weeks before the competition, Mr. Callaghan suggested that we replace the triple salchow–triple loop combination in my long program with a triple loop–triple loop combination.

I gave him a look. Triple loop–triple loop combinations are very tough. I wasn't sure I could pull one off.

"Let's just try," Mr. Callaghan said. "Because if you can handle the new combination, your technical scores will improve."

That sounded interesting!

"Okay," I agreed. "I'll try it." Inside, I had already decided to go after the combination one hundred percent.

Mr. Callaghan talked me through the jump combination.

I landed the very first one I tried! But there was a lot of room for improvement. Mr. Callaghan gave me some pointers.

I tried the jump combination again. And again. Sometimes I fell. Sometimes I "popped" one of the jumps, substituting a double for a triple at the last second. And then—*pow!* I did a beautiful triple loop–triple loop.

Mr. Callaghan and I both started smiling. I was really amazed. He had been right. I *could* do it.

"That wasn't so hard," he said.

I shook my head.

"Now we just have to get the new combination into your program."

That proved more challenging. Sometimes I landed the combination, and then the next time I'd fall or pop into a simpler combination. But over the next two weeks I kept practicing, so that by the time we left for Philadelphia, I felt comfortable with the triple loop–triple loop. Now all I had to do was land it in the competition.

The United States Postal Service Challenge was a pretty ritzy event. It was held in the brand new CoreStates center in Philadelphia, and lots of skating stars were there to compete as part of organized teams. I was on a team with Dorothy Hamill, Michelle Kwan, Dan Hollander, and Caryn Kadavy. We were skating against another team made up of Todd Eldredge, Paul Wylie, Tonia Kwiatkowski, and Rosalynn Sumners.

With all these Olympic and world medalists around, no one was paying much attention to me. That is, not until I landed my triple loop–triple loop. I became the first skater—woman or man—to land a triple loop–triple loop at a meet.

The reporters were suddenly buzzing around me. "How long did you practice the combination?" someone wanted to know.

"Two weeks," I said.

The reporters thought I was crazy. But what could I say? It was true!

14

NATIONAL CHAMPION

I was a bundle of nerves at the 1997 Nationals!

Being nervous goes hand in hand with competing, but when my parents, Mr. Callaghan, and I got to Nashville for the competition, I was *super* nervous. To help calm myself down, I did all the stuff I usually do to get ready—checked over my dresses, talked to my friends, and visualized my programs in my mind. Doing that stuff usually soothes my nerves and helps me focus. But this time it wasn't working.

On the Wednesday before the competition, I went to the Vanderbilt Children's Hospital to visit. Since it was right before Valentine's Day, I brought little valentines to pass out. The kids loved it. I was the only one having a hard time relaxing and enjoying myself.

I kept thinking about the competition. All the top American women in the sport had gathered in Nashville, and Mr. Callaghan thought four of us had a good chance at the top three spots: Nicole Bobek, Michelle Kwan, Tonia Kwiatkowski (who had finished eighth in the world the year before), and me. To make the World team, I was going to have to skate better than at least one of them.

For some reason, I got more and more nervous. I'm not quite sure where that feeling came from. My training in Detroit couldn't have been stronger. I had done well in the fall championship series. And I had been skating well in practice all week. Still, I just couldn't calm down.

On Friday—the day we were supposed to skate the short program—Mr. Callaghan spent extra time talking to me. I was beyond precompetition jitters. I was so nervous I thought something might be wrong with me.

Mr. Callaghan assured me nothing was wrong. He reminded me that I'd been nervous at the Nationals the year before. It was normal. As with every

Nationals, it was time to test my technical, artistic, and mental abilities against those of the best American skaters.

Mr. Callaghan also told me that being nervous might even help me skate better.

Our talk reassured me, and I was determined to keep my nerves under control.

A phone call I received also helped. It was from the famous gymnastics coach Bela Karolyi. Mr. Karolyi phoned me at my hotel that afternoon. His advice sounded a lot like Mr. Callaghan's—he told me to just go out and skate the way I had every day in practice. It was an honor to talk to him, and knowing that he and so many people were behind me helped put me in a much better mental state.

Being in the right mental state when you're competing is crucial. And even though spectators always think I seem calm and collected when the pressure is on, controlling my emotions is something I'm still struggling with. For example, I've learned that it's important for me to have a goal when I go into a competition. Without one, I don't try my hardest. At the Nationals, my goal was to come in third.

But if I'm *too* focused on my goal, I get all nervous and my muscles tense up and nothing works. So while I try to set a goal and push myself to meet it, I also try to remember that I'll always have another chance.

By the time Friday night finally rolled around, I was much calmer. I kept reminding myself that if I didn't come in third, there would always be next year. I skated my short program, and it went really smoothly. I was *so* glad to be finished with the first part of the competition. My scores were pretty good, too. I ended up in second place.

On Saturday the pace of the competition picked up. The men skated their long programs in the afternoon. Todd placed first after the short program and held on to win the men's title after the long program. I was really proud of him, but he wasn't happy with his performance. And he calls me a perfectionist! I think Todd skated great, but I respect him for having such high standards.

After the men finished, I started to get ready for my long program.

By the time the first of the women glided onto the ice, the Nashville Arena was packed with sixteen thousand extremely enthusiastic spectators. ABC Sports was covering the event. Television viewers across the nation were tuned in. My parents were there—somewhere up in the sold-out stands. Todd was watching on a television monitor in the athletes' lounge.

I was in a very up mood. My second-place finish the day before had boosted my confidence. I had the usual competition nervousness, but the extreme jitters I'd experienced earlier in the week were gone.

I reminded myself that if I wanted to go to the Worlds, I'd have to nail my long program. Even though I was currently in second place, Nicole, Tonia, and plenty of other terrific skaters would be trying to slip by me and snag the chance to go to Switzerland. There was no room for mistakes.

After we had all warmed up, I changed back into my running shoes. I had to skate last in my group, which for me isn't the greatest. I prefer to skate earlier, but I tried not to worry about it.

While the other competitors took their turns, I hung out in the locker room. I jogged in place to keep my muscles warm. And I tried to stay focused. Todd came out of the skaters' lounge. "It's just like every day in practice," he told me. "Go out and do your thing and you'll be fine."

"Thanks," I whispered, grateful for his advice and encouragement.

Finally it was almost my turn. I walked over to the ice. When I got to the boards, Michelle had just finished skating. As she came off the ice, I noticed that she didn't look at all happy.

Mr. Callaghan hurried up to me. "Okay, Tara," he said. "Just pretend it's another day at the rink."

I nodded. Mr. Callaghan always tells me the same thing right before I compete. It helps, but it's hard to pretend it's just another day at the rink when sixteen thousand people are crowded into the stands.

I started to step onto the ice, but Mr. Callaghan pulled me back.

"What's wrong?" I asked.

"Just wait a second," he replied.

I noticed what was bothering him. The crowd was booing.

"They're not booing at you," Mr. Callaghan reassured me.

No, it seemed as if the crowd was reacting to

Michelle's scores, which had just come up. I looked at them too. They *weren't* great, and I was a little confused. (Later I found out that Michelle had fallen three times during her program. She'd had a bad day.)

Of course, I knew instantly what that meant. If I skated really well, I might win!

Mr. Callaghan seemed to read my mind. "Don't try to win," he told me firmly. "Just do your work."

His words didn't surprise me. I remembered my experience at the Worlds the year before, when I'd gotten distracted by my thoughts about beating Midori Ito, had pushed too hard, had ruined the timing of my jumps, and had landed on my backside—several times. Big mistake.

So I tried to put the chance of winning out of my mind, and instead I concentrated on my program. When the crowd calmed down, I glided onto the ice. My music began to play. I started to skate.

My first jump was a double axel. I brought my arms in and my right leg up and thrust myself into the air. Tucking in tight, I spun around two and a half times before I came down.

My triple flip was next. It was huge! By then I was getting into the rhythm of my program. And the audience rewarded me by clapping loudly.

Next came my triple Lutz–double toe loop. I nailed it!

The tempo of my music slowed. I had time to catch my breath. But I couldn't relax yet. My next combination was a tricky one: the triple loop–triple loop.

I pushed off the edge of my skate and flew into the first triple loop. I came down cleanly. So far, so good. Almost immediately I pushed off into my second jump, spun around one, two, three times, and landed solidly.

A cheer went up from the crowd. I started to smile. My program was going really well. And the crowd's support kept me psyched.

The rest of my program went by in a blur, but every jump and spin felt good. When I finished, the crowd went wild. They rose to their feet and applauded madly. It was a moment I'll never forget.

I was ecstatic. I had skated my very best.

Mr. Callaghan was waiting for me at the edge of the ice. "Great job, Tara!" he told me.

"Thanks," I said, beaming.

We walked over to the kiss and cry area, the nickname skaters have for the bench where you wait for your scores. We call it that because if you've skated well, everyone kisses each other; if you've skated badly, everyone cries.

Pretty soon my scores came up. At first I couldn't believe them! None of the judges gave me a mark lower than 5.8. Plus, I'd earned six technical marks of 5.9 and three artistic 5.9s. In other words . . .

I'd won! I was the new U.S. Ladies Singles Champion!

15

INTO THE LIMELIGHT

Tara Lipinski—U.S. Ladies Singles Champion.

The fact that I'd won didn't really sink in until the next morning.

I knew I owed a small part of my victory to luck because by not skating well, Michelle Kwan had opened a door for me. But I owed a bigger part of my victory to dedication, focus, and plain hard work. All the hours of practice had helped me to skate through that door.

My parents, my relatives, my friends, Todd, Mr. Callaghan—everyone was thrilled for me. I was proud that I had accomplished something so amazing at such a young age. But with the victory in Nashville, I was also under more pressure. The Worlds were only about a month away. Millions of people would be watching to see how I'd do.

I tried to put that scary thought out of my mind as Mom and I flew off to New York on a victory tour. Todd was there too!

Tons of reporters wanted to talk to me. *People* magazine published an article about me and put a small picture of me on the cover.

One morning we left the hotel at five-forty-five to tape an interview for *This Morning* and then zipped across town to appear live on *Good Morning, America.* Seeing a live television show in action was totally cool, especially *Good Morning, America,* since that's a show I sometimes watch while I'm stretching in the morning. I couldn't believe how small the set looked in real life.

The next day I went to a taping of *Late Night with David Letterman!* We were invited to sit in the green room during the show. The green room is where guests hang out while they're waiting for their turn with Dave. In case you're wondering, the room is not painted green, so I'm not sure why they call it a green room. Maybe it's because people are nervous and get sick to their stomachs while they're waiting.

While we were there I met Jeff Gordon, the youngest race car driver ever to win the Daytona 500. I also got my picture taken with Dave.

While we were in New York, Mom and I made time to stop by the offices of the fashion designer Donna Karan. Ms. Karan had supplied the USA World team with really cool DKNY warm-up gear. I especially liked the bright red, shiny jacket. It was nice to get to thank Ms. Karan in person, but I felt a little shy around her.

All the excitement was terrific. And I loved being in New York. It's definitely one of my favorite cities. But I kept thinking about what winning the Nationals really meant. I was going to the Worlds. And before I could even think about that, I had the International Skating Union's championship final. That competition was only ten days away.

So when I was invited to fly to Chicago and

appear on *Oprah,* I said, "Thanks, but no thanks." With two big competitions looming, I knew I had to get home and get back to my training routine. So Mom and I boarded a plane for Detroit. I hope I'll get another chance to do *Oprah.*

16

ANOTHER IMPORTANT WIN

My life definitely changed the day I won the Nationals. But Mr. Callaghan encouraged me not to dwell on my new title or any of the amazing things that were happening to me. At least, not until we got through the last two competitions of the season. He also wanted my training schedule to stay the same. I agreed completely. In fact, I was anxious to return to my routine.

After I got back from New York, Mr. Callaghan and I concentrated on getting in as much training as possible before the Champions Series Final in Hamilton, Ontario, Canada. I had earned my spot in the competition by doing well at Skate Canada and Trophée Lalique earlier in the season.

The Champions Series Final was exciting because it was a big, important international competition. Plus, after my big win at the Nationals, the spotlight was definitely on me. Skating fans across the country were waiting to see if I could handle my new celebrity and execute a world-class performance.

Still, I didn't pressure myself to win. My goal was to place in the top three. But I did much better than that—I took first.

Winning at the Series Final was satisfying because it showed everyone that my victory at the Nationals wasn't a one-time thing. Also, I felt reassured that I had done the right thing to end my victory tour early.

But there was no time to stand around patting myself on the back. The Worlds were only a few weeks away.

17

WORLD CHAMPION

My mother, Mr. Callaghan, and I took off for Lausanne on the Wednesday before the Worlds. My father was booked on a flight the following week. I was glad that both my parents would be there to share this exciting experience.

As soon as we arrived in Lausanne on Thursday morning, we checked into our hotel. We had hoped to have a practice session that day, but the organizers had scheduled my ice time for eleven *at night*. Not a good way to beat jet lag! Mr. Callaghan quickly decided that a decent night's sleep was more important than practicing.

I was glad to have the night off because I had a cold. I couldn't wait to get to bed.

The next morning I woke up feeling better. Mom and I checked out our surroundings. The city of Lausanne is really pretty. Shops and restaurants are scattered everywhere, and Lake Geneva is beautiful. We did a little clothes shopping and stopped at a café.

When we went to the arena, I was surprised by its size. It had only six thousand seats. Since I love a big crowd, I was a little disappointed. But then I reminded myself that millions more people would be watching the competition on TV. That's a big enough crowd—even for me!

Starting on Friday, Mr. Callaghan and I established a routine: two practices each day for about forty-five minutes each time. One practice in the morning and one in the afternoon. We did that on Saturday and Sunday too.

By Monday—the day the qualifying rounds took place—I was over my jet lag, and my cold was nearly gone. I felt ready to skate!

Starting in 1997 every skater had to fulfill a new International Skating Union rule. *Everyone* had to qualify at the Worlds—even Todd, who was the men's champion the year before! For the qualifying round, the competition organizers split us up into two groups and had us skate our long programs. The top thirty women out of a field of forty-three went on to compete.

I didn't mind qualifying. I looked at it as an opportunity to get warmed up for the real competition. I felt very focused as I glided onto the ice and took my opening position.

I broke into a big smile as I started to skate. It felt great to be on the ice in front of the judges. I skated well and placed first in my group! Nicole Bobek was second, and the Russian skater Maria Butyrskaya was third.

Winning in the qualifying rounds doesn't really count for anything, but it did give my confidence a big boost.

Going into the Worlds, I didn't set the goal of winning. I'd won two competitions in a row, and I knew that nobody can stay on top forever. All I wanted to do was to improve on my placement at the Worlds the year before. Placing fifth, or eighth, or anything better than fifteenth would have made me happy.

The next few days were really difficult. After the qualifying round, I felt as if I was on a roll. I wanted the competition to keep going. Instead, we had three days of downtime before we skated our short programs on Friday evening. The Worlds were the longest competition of the year—they stretched over an entire week.

Keeping focused all that time was difficult. But Mr. Callaghan and I stuck to our schedule. One practice in the morning, one practice in the afternoon. After we had finished at the arena for the day, I ate dinner, then went back to the hotel to watch some television.

The men skated on Wednesday and Thursday. I watched as much of their events as I could and saw a lot of great skating. Especially from Todd, Elvis Stojko, and the Russians.

By Thursday I was starting to have a hard time concentrating during practice. I wanted to skate for real! All the waiting was making me nervous. I was particularly worried about my short program. I kept thinking about the way I had blown it the year before—and hoped it wasn't some sort of short-program-at-the-Worlds jinx.

Friday morning I had my last practice before the short program.

I was starting to get seriously jittery!

Mr. Callaghan reminded me that my nervousness had actually ended up helping me win at the Nationals. I decided not to try to fight it.

But then two terrible things happened that really brought down the mood of the American delegation.

Word reached us that Carlo Fassi, Nicole Bobek's coach, had died suddenly from a heart attack.

Mr. Fassi was a great skating coach. He trained four Olympic gold medalists: Peggy Fleming, Dorothy Hamill, John Curry, and Robin Cousins. Mr. Callaghan didn't say much about Mr. Fassi's death, but I knew he was shaken up. They had worked together in Colorado for two years and knew each other well. Mr. Fassi's death was especially hard because we had seen him, looking healthy, just a few hours before.

We also learned that Scott Hamilton, the 1984 Olympic gold medalist, had cancer. I've always looked up to Scott, and the idea that he was suffering made me sad. Focusing during practice that afternoon was impossible, and I skated just as badly as I felt.

But the competition didn't stop. Later that day it was time to put my sad feelings aside and go out and do my work.

Last to skate again? I thought after we had picked our places for the short program. It seemed as if I had been last more than my fair share in competitions that season. But then I reminded myself that skating last hadn't hurt me at Nationals, and I stopped worrying about it. After my group warmed up, I went back into the locker rooms. *Focus,* I told myself as the minutes ticked by. I tried not to think about what was happening on the ice until it was my turn.

Finally I found myself waiting in the center of the rink for my music to begin.

I went into my first element: a layback spin. I got a good arch in my back and spun faster and faster. Then I came out of the layback and moved into my spiral sequence. That felt good too. I extended my leg nicely and remembered to move my arms gracefully—just as Marina had taught me.

The music sped up as I prepared for my first jump—a triple Lutz–double loop combination. It felt solid. I landed cleanly and then immediately tapped my foot, scooped my arms in, and catapulted back into the air. I came down into another clean landing. Yes! My routine was going great.

Next came my flying camel, which was no problem. I picked up speed and then moved into my triple flip. I bent one knee and reached back with my other toe. I pushed my toe picks into the ice and snapped my legs and arms together. I sprang into the air—and the next thing I knew I was safely down. Only one more jump to go: my double axel.

I skated around and then popped back up into the air. The two and a half revolutions passed in a heartbeat. My program was almost over. I did my footwork and then a combination spin.

The audience applauded as I finished my program.

I felt like applauding too! After my terrible short program the year before at the Worlds, I ended up taking first.

Michelle also skated well. But she stumbled coming out of the triple Lutz in her combination. She came in fourth.

Irina Slutskaya was sixth.

We skated our long programs on Saturday evening.

Nicole Bobek was in the group before me, so I didn't see her skate. But I later found out that she had knelt on the ice at the end of her program and had said a prayer for Carlo Fassi. Finishing the competition was very brave of her. I can't imagine how she was able to go through with it.

I ended up with the second spot in my group, which I was glad about. I was on the ice before I had a chance to get keyed up. And I was off just as quickly. My program went by in a flash. It felt so great that I wished it could have lasted longer!

"Awesome!" Mr. Callaghan said as I came off the ice.

Time for kiss and cry! Mr. Callaghan, Megan Faulkner, and I sat down to wait for my scores. My program had *felt* terrific. I just hoped it had *looked* as good to the judges.

It must have because my technical marks were all 5.8s and 5.9s. Mr. Callaghan was even happier to see my artistic scores. The Japanese and Italian judges had given me artistic marks that were just as high as the technical ones. And the Polish judge had even gone *up* on my artistic mark—and awarded me a 5.9. All our hard work on my "sophistication" over the past year had paid off. I knew Marina and Sandra would be proud too!

Then Mr. Callaghan, Megan, and I settled down to watch the rest of the skaters. I felt a little self-conscious because each time someone's scores were posted, the television cameras zoomed in on my face to get my reaction. I tried to keep smiling.

Michelle skated a strong long program.

Irina, who skated last, was also good, especially since she had fallen and crashed into the boards earlier in the day. But she dropped one of her triple jumps.

The scoring for the long program was *super* close! Michelle and I each received three first-place ordinals. To break the tie, the officials added the number of first- *and* second-place ordinals we'd been awarded. It turned out that Michelle came in first for the long program and I came in second. That was good enough for me to hold on to my overall lead.

Winning was a real shock. Everyone had skated

well, which made the competition more intense and ultimately made winning an extra-super thrill.

Someone told me that fifteen of the past eighteen world champions have gone on to win the next year's Olympics! Next year should be very interesting.

Epilogue

Triumph on Ice

Spring 1998

Interesting?

The next year turned out to be much more than simply interesting. It was magical, satisfying, joyous, and completely unforgettable. That's because 1998 was the year my fondest dream came true. It was the year I became an Olympic champion.

My Olympic experience began on February 7, 1998, when I marched into Ceremony Stadium in Nagano, Japan, as one member of the huge U.S. delegation. As I marched, I waved at the thousands of enthusiastic spectators. They responded by snapping photographs, aiming video cameras my way, and cheering.

All my life I'd dreamed of competing in the Olympic Games—and now here I was! *No matter what else happens in my life,* I thought, *competing in the Olympics will be a highlight.*

I wasn't the only one looking forward to the next few weeks of skating competition. The rest of the American women's delegation—Michelle Kwan and Nicole Bobek—were very strong skaters. Nicole and Michelle hadn't even arrived in Japan yet, and reporters were already buzzing about the possibility of an American medal sweep. They were saying I would take the silver. But I wasn't paying too much attention to the media's predictions. I was listening to my heart, and the medal it wanted was gold.

As we marched, I glanced at the American delegation. Todd and skater Michael Weiss were at my side. Beyond them were dozens of other American athletes—speed skaters, hockey players, skiers, and snowboarders. They were all smiling under their official cowboy hats. They all looked excited. I felt incredibly lucky to be part of such a talented group of people.

And I was able to share the opening ceremony with more than just my teammates. CBS Sports had put a microphone on my jacket. As we paraded around the stadium, I talked to everyone watching back home. I told them, "I want to remember this moment forever."

There were other moments in 1998 I wouldn't mind *forgetting*. For example, the January evening I skated my short program at the Nationals. My program was going really well until I took off for my triple flip, missed my landing, and fell. The audience moaned in disappointment.

I was disappointed too. My crash landing dropped me to fourth place. I hardly ever fall during competitions. But, looking back, I guess that fall was almost predictable. You can't skate well unless your mind is in the right place. During the Nationals, my mind wasn't on the competition. It was in Sewell, New Jersey.

Remember when I told you about my aunt Edith? Well, one thing I didn't mention was that she needed a liver transplant. She'd been waiting for a new liver for almost ten years. Now her health was deteriorating badly, and nobody knew whether she would get a transplant in time to save her life.

Concentrating on skating is tough when someone you love is desperately ill. So there I was, competing for one of three spots on the Olympic team—and in fourth place after the short program.

At that point, lots of people thought I wouldn't make the Olympics. But I don't give up easily. I fought back with a strong, clean long program and ended up taking second. My spot on the Olympic team was secured.

Aunt Edith is a fighter too. She held on during those last cold days in January, and even kept her spirits up. One night she dreamed that she got her new liver and I won a gold medal in the Olympics. We both hoped the dream was a premonition of wonderful things to come.

And it was! Aunt Edith got her new liver on the same day Mom and I boarded a plane for Nagano. When we got to Japan, we learned that Aunt Edith's operation had gone well. I was so happy and relieved. A cloud lifted, and I suddenly realized I was about to start the most exciting competition of my life.

The Olympics are special for many reasons.

For one thing, they're huge. The Nagano Games

featured seven sports with three thousand competitors from seventy-two countries. Thousands of spectators were on hand to watch the Games, with millions more tuned in on TV. So much was going on that the entire town seemed to pulse with excitement.

Also, unlike the Nationals or Worlds, the Olympics take place only once every four years. If you mess up at a competition like the Nationals, you can tell yourself, "I'll do better next year." But it's not so easy to predict what will happen in *four* years.

Going into Nagano, I knew this Olympic experience might be my *only* Olympic experience. That's why I arrived at the games in time to march in the opening ceremony. And that's why I decided to stay in the Olympic Village with the other athletes. I wanted to squeeze every experience I could out of the Games. I wanted to live the Olympics.

My friend Todd Eldredge is one skater who managed to come back for a second Olympics. Todd finished tenth at the 1992 Games in Albertville. This time he was determined to take home a medal. On the evening of the men's short program, I was in the stands to cheer him on.

Todd skated well. So did Russia's Ilya Kulik and Canada's Elvis Stojko. The scoring was close, and none of the skaters received more than four first-place ordinals. Todd ended up third. He and Mr. Callaghan both believed he still had a good chance for a gold medal.

The next night I was back in the stands to watch the men's long program. Ilya Kulik skated first and turned in a performance that would be hard to beat. I held my breath as Todd took the ice. I knew this was likely to be Todd's last Olympics—and I wanted to see my teammate and friend up on the podium receiving a medal.

The beginning of Todd's program was clean, but near the end, he singled one of his triple jumps. He must have been trying to make up for that when he attempted to turn his double axel into a triple—and fell.

I told myself the bronze medal was still within Todd's reach. But that hope faded when France's Philippe Candeloro skated a great program and nudged into third place.

Naturally, Todd was disappointed with his fourth-place finish—not just because of the medal but because he hadn't skated his best. But Todd has been in hundreds of competitions, and he knows that sometimes things just don't go the way you'd like.

When you think about it, things *have* gone Todd's way lots of times. He has a world championship and five national championships to prove it.

Four days later Todd and I switched places. Now he was the one cheering—and I was the one waiting for my turn on the ice.

As my time to compete in the short program crept closer and closer, I had the usual precompetition jitters—times two. After all, this was the Olympics! After years of training, I had two minutes and forty seconds to show the world what I could do.

That nervousness might have gotten out of hand if I hadn't felt surrounded by so much support.

My decision to stay in the Olympic Village was definitely a good one. Being there reminded me that I was just one of many athletes competing in the

Games. That sense of community relieved a lot of the pressure.

Then there was my family. I knew Aunt Edith, Uncle Phil, and all my cousins were watching the Games on TV back home. Mom and Dad were right there in White Ring arena, hiding from the cameras somewhere up in the overflowing stands.

I knew my friends, including Erin Elbe, had their fingers crossed for me.

And then there were my coaches. Mr. Callaghan and Megan stayed close by and offered many words of encouragement.

By the time I stepped onto the ice, I was excited about performing my short program for the judges and everyone who was watching.

I skated to music from the movie *Anastasia*. If you've seen it, you know what a brave character Anastasia is. The music is great because I think of her bravery while I skate and it gives me courage.

The music began. I stretched into my layback, gracefully moving my arms through the air.

If I live to be 100, I'll never forget this program. Especially not the sections that allow me to show my artistry. Over the previous year, I had spent hundreds of hours refining the way I looked on the ice. While I was traveling with the Tour of World Figure Skating Champions over the summer of 1997, I studied how the other skaters moved their arms and held their heads. Later I spent time in front of a mirror, perfecting my own moves and working to connect with the audience.

Now, when it counted most, all that hard work paid off. My layback felt right on. And so did the spiral sequence that followed.

I skated around and started to pick up speed— another part of the performance I'd been working on. Moving quickly makes a skater look confident and leads to high scores. I sped across the ice and went into a triple Lutz-double loop combination.

Both jumps were solid.

Next I did a flying camel, remembering to extend my back leg fully. I forced myself to concentrate on the footwork that came next. It felt smooth as silk.

Again I picked up speed. I gave my toe pick a strong push and popped up into a quick triple flip.

The flip was the jump I had crash-landed at the Nationals. This time I landed cleanly.

What a relief! I broke into a smile. Now I was having fun—but I still had some business to attend to. There was one more jump to go: the double axel. I skated into position and pushed off. I rotated two and a half times—and nailed the landing!

I smiled all the way through my final footwork and combination spin. At the end I threw my arms out the way I always do. But this time the motion didn't just signal the completion of my program; it signaled a feeling of satisfaction. I couldn't remember ever feeling stronger.

The crowd cheered wildly. They tossed stuffed animals and flowers onto the ice. I stood in the middle of the rink, lingering much longer than usual, not wanting the moment to end. Finally, though, I skated over to where Mr. Callaghan was waiting.

"I did it!" I told him.

"Big-time, you did it!" Mr. Callaghan's face was lit up with a triumphant smile.

"That was my best performance ever!" I said

with disbelief. I was so happy with the way I had skated that I felt like laughing and crying all at once.

I had a hard time sitting still in the kiss and cry area. But my scores were worth the wait. I even got a first placement for artistry from the French judge! Mr. Callaghan told me that he had never seen me skate a more graceful program.

As soon as I left the kiss and cry area, I pulled on my warm-ups and ran into the stands to join my teammates. For now, I was in first place. All I had to do was wait and see how everyone else skated.

Nicole Bobek was the next American to take the ice. Almost immediately I could tell that she was having a rough time. She fell on her triple Lutz and doubled out of a triple toe loop. I knew that Nicole had been sick the previous week, and I wondered if that was making her weak.

"There go our chances for a sweep," someone commented.

I nodded, feeling bad for Nicole. I'd had a similar experience back at the Edmonton Worlds, and I remembered how angry I'd been at myself for performing poorly.

Unlike Nicole, Michelle delivered a clean program and ended up in first place. I was second. Russian Maria Butyrskaya was third, and China's Lu Chen was fourth.

In just two days we would all compete for the gold.

The long program was scheduled for February twentieth. The next day was my mother's birthday. My father's birthday was just three days after that. I thought a gold medal would make a nice double birthday present.

But by then my excitement over how well I'd skated in the short program was wearing off and my nervousness was creeping back in. That afternoon I hung out in the Olympic Village, played in the game room, and tried to soak up some confidence from my fellow athletes.

People were still expecting me to take the silver. Reporters were saying I could win only if Michelle fell. Mr. Callaghan didn't agree. He told me the winner would be the one who was the most aggressive on the ice. A safe, comfortable program wasn't going to be enough. If I wanted a gold medal, I had to skate with all my heart.

During dinner in my parents' hotel room that evening, Mom and I huddled for our usual pre-competition quiet time.

"I think I'm scared," I confessed.

Mom was quiet for a long moment. "You have a right to be scared," she finally said. "But you're going to do it. Just believe in your prayers and in St. Theresa."

Thinking about St. Theresa at that moment was incredibly calming. Mom and I have been praying to St. Theresa for years, and I believe she has helped my skating immensely. I know she's with me when I'm competing, and that makes me feel ready to give my all.

I gave Mom a kiss, gathered my stuff, and left. But I'd only gotten a few steps down the hallway when I turned around and came back. I found Mom sitting in the same spot, looking nervous.

"I can do it, Mom," I told her. "Happy birthday."

When I left the room the second time, Mom was smiling.

I'd drawn the fifth skating position—not the greatest spot for me. Going fifth gives your muscles plenty of time to cool down after the warm-up. It also gives your nerves plenty of time to get jittery.

Immediately after the warm-up, I went back into a practice room to pull on my sweats. I jogged around in circles and did stretches to keep my muscles warm. The exercise also helped me stay calm and focused.

Meanwhile, Michelle, who was first in our group, was taking the ice out in the main rink. I didn't watch her skate. Mr. Callaghan and I left the arena and went into the practice rink, so I couldn't hear the scores. Before I skated, Mr. Callaghan told me that Michelle hadn't made any major mistakes.

Michelle hadn't left the door open for me the way she had at the 1997 Nationals, but I was determined to wiggle through even the smallest crack. I was actually glad Michelle had skated well. I didn't want to win because she'd had an off night. I wanted to beat her at the top of her form.

Lu Chen skated. Then Maria Butyrskaya and Surya Bonaly.

Finally it was my turn!

I went out to the rink and got into position on the ice. While I waited for my music to begin, I had a second to soak up the atmosphere of White Ring. The arena was beautiful, especially the wonderful soft lights.

This is it, I thought. *Enjoy it.*

The first section of my music, from the movie *The Rainbow,* came on. I chose that piece because it evokes strong emotions in me. The music tells the story of a young woman growing up and finding out what she loves and believes in. I feel as though my skating is teaching me the same things.

I moved into my first element, a layback. Next I did a quick, tight double axel. I got good height on the jump and felt loose and warmed up.

Next came the triple flip. Everything felt right on, including the landing.

I skated around and gained some speed for my first combination, a triple Lutz-double toe loop. The jumps felt good.

The first part of my program was already over.

My music slowed into a selection from *Scenes of Summer*. This slow part lets me catch my breath and gives me time to show the judges my artistry.

I moved into my footwork, feeling incredibly happy to be at the Olympics and skating well. That emotion helped me get into the music and almost dance through this lyrical section. I was trying to connect with the judges, the audience, the world.

Now the rhythm of the music picked up and I skated faster, gaining speed for my triple loop-triple loop combination. The triple loop-triple loop is still my signature move. This one was the best I've ever landed in competition.

Once I got through that, I knew a great performance was within reach. *Don't think about winning now!* I told myself. I had to calm down and do my work. One stupid mistake would ruin everything.

I did a camel and a back camel. Then I sped across the ice, getting ready for my second triple Lutz. I guess that on some level, I remembered what Mr. Callaghan had said about being aggressive. I held nothing back, and the Lutz was strong.

Only one more combination to go: a triple toe-half loop-triple salchow.

This is a difficult combination even at the beginning of a program when your legs are fresh, but mine comes just seconds before the end, when I've already been skating for almost four minutes. That combination pushes my technical marks way up because it shows the judges the strength I have.

I pushed off my toe pick and soared into the air. One, two, three rotations, and then I was down cleanly. I pushed off again, flipping quickly through the half turn. Now I was in position for my salchow. Almost immediately I sprang up off the back inside edge of my left foot, rotated three times, and landed on the back outside edge of my right foot.

By now the crowd was starting to go wild. As I went through the final elements in my program, I felt overwhelmed. I had just skated the program of my life in the most important competition in my life.

I struck my final pose. But I was only able to hold it for a few seconds. I was bursting with so much happy energy that I raced across the ice, wishing I knew how to embrace the moment and hold on to it forever.

The memory of my final performance in White Ring—the crowd, the beautiful lights, and my joy—will be with me always. But the actual moment went by in a flash. Too soon, it was time for me to get off the ice and give another skater her turn.

As I moved over to the kiss and cry area, Megan and Mr. Callaghan looked just as amazed and proud as I felt. I started to sob with relief and happiness. Then, when I saw my scores, I jumped to my feet and shrieked with elation.

I knew immediately that my scores were high enough to put me in first place. I had won!

No more than fifteen minutes later, I was standing on top of a podium, clutching flowers and feeling the wonderful weight of an Olympic gold medal around my neck.

The national anthem swelled and the crowd began to sing.

I felt so good. I'd completed a journey I'd begun

when I was just two years old. And let me tell you, a real Olympic podium definitely beats Tupperware!

As I looked out at the crowd and up at the flag, everything was perfect. My Olympic dream had come true.

My Favorite Things

Colors: Blue and purple—definitely *not* orange!

Skaters: Todd Eldredge, Kurt Browning, Kristi Yamaguchi

Nonskating athlete: Dominique Moceanu

Male entertainers: Scott Wolf, Matthew Perry, Tom Cruise, David Letterman

Female entertainers: Lacey Chabert, Neve Campbell, Jennifer Aniston, Rosie O'Donnell

TV shows: *Party of Five; Friends; Today; Wheel of Fortune; Late Night with David Letterman*

Foods: Pizza, steak, pasta with tomato sauce, salad, grapes, Oreo-cookie brownies (my specialty!)

Least favorite food/beverage/condiment: Broccoli, water, mustard

Music: Alternative

Animals: Frogs and dogs—especially my family's golden retriever, Brandy, our two bichon frises, Camelot and Lancelot, our Yorkshire terrier, Mischief, and our Maltese, Coco

Jewelry: My World team ring. My many necklace charms: a skate with "Thumbs Up" written on it that Uncle Phil gave me, one that says "Short but Good," another that says "USA," plus a St. Theresa medallion.

Clothes: Shoes, shoes, and more shoes!

Car: Any car I'll be able to drive once I get my license.

Storybook character: Snow White

Vacation spot: Walt Disney World. I've been there ten times!

Magazines: *Teen* and *Seventeen*

Book: *All Creatures Great and Small* by James Herriot

Web site: Mine! The address is http://www.taralipinski.com. I love getting e-mail from all my fans.

Guide to Scoring in Figure Skating

by Emily Costello

Combinations, Lutzes, spiral sequences—sometimes when you watch Tara skate on television, it seems as if the commentators are speaking a foreign language. Especially when they talk about scoring. All you want to know is who's ahead, but the folks on TV are jabbering about ordinals and factors and other mysterious things. If you're a regular non-skating human being, you probably end up feeling pretty confused.

Well, your confusion is about to end! Think of the following guide as your Ice-Skating-to-English dictionary. The guide will help you understand what's happening on the ice so that you'll have more fun when you watch skating.

THE SECRETS OF SCORING

Ice skating combines athletic jumps and spins with graceful movement. That's what makes skating such fun to watch. Unfortunately, that mix of sport and art also makes scoring a bit tricky. It's not a matter of hitting the most home runs or shooting the most baskets. Who wins in skating is based solely on the judges' opinions.

Poor judges! They have a hard job. Assigning a score to a skater's performance is a little like judging a ballet or a painting. Audiences who dislike the scores a skater receives have been known to boo judges or accuse them of playing favorites. But even if the scoring seems unfair at times, ice skating does have its rules. Here's an overview of Tara's division, ladies' singles:

LADIES' SINGLES

Competitors in the singles division compete in two events: the technical, or short, program, and the free skate or long program.

The Short Program

In this event, a skater performs certain required elements to music of her own choosing. The required moves change each season, but here's an up-to-date list:

a double axel

a double or triple jump

a double-triple or triple-triple jump combination (two jumps without a step in between)

a flying spin

a layback or sideways-leaning spin

a spin combination with one change of foot and at least two changes of position

two sequences of steps or footwork done in either a straight line or a circle

After skating, the competitor receives two marks from each judge. The first mark is for required elements—how well the moves were executed. The second mark is for artistic impression. In determining artistic scores, the judges examine many different things. They consider the skater's use of the rink; the skater's speed and confidence; the program's degree of daring; the height, spacing, and variety of jumps; and the overall presentation.

The judges' marks range from 0.0 to 6.0, based on the following scale:

0—not skated

1—very poor

2—poor

3—average

4—good

5—excellent

6—perfect

Decimal points help the judges make the scores precise. For example, a skater might receive a score of 3.8, 4.2, or 5.5.

After the scores are announced, an official combines the two scores from each judge. This combined score is compared with the scores given by that same judge to the other competitors and ranked best, second best, and so on. These rankings are called ordinals. The skater who has the most first-place ordinals after everyone has skated wins the short program.

Still confused? Maybe an example will help!

		JUDGES						
		1	2	3	4	5	6	7
Skater	Required	5.9	5.8	5.7	5.8	5.8	5.7	5.8
A	Artistic	5.8	5.8	5.8	5.9	5.7	5.6	5.8
	TOTAL	11.7	11.6	11.5	11.7	11.5	11.3	11.6
Skater	Required	5.7	5.6	5.7	5.8	5.7	5.6	5.7
B	Artistic	5.6	5.6	5.7	5.6	5.8	5.7	5.8
	TOTAL	11.3	11.2	11.4	11.4	11.5	11.3	11.5

Who wins? Skater A. Why? Because her combined scores are the highest given by each judge five out of seven times. Or, if you prefer to use skater lingo, she has five first-place ordinals.

But the short program is worth only one third of the skater's overall score. Skaters say that the short program has a factor of .5. That means the officials multiply the skater's placement (*not* her score) by .5 to determine the placement's worth in terms of the overall competition. A skater who finishes first earns a factored score of .5 ($1 \times .5 = .5$); a second-place finisher gets a factored score of 1 ($2 \times .5 = 1$), and so on.

The Long Program

The long program is sometimes called the free skate because there are no required elements. The only rule is that women's programs must last four minutes.

The scoring is the same as in the short program, except that instead of receiving scores for required elements, skaters are judged on technical merit. At the end, each skater's placement in the long program is added to her factored placement in the short program. Whoever has the *lowest* overall placement is the winner.

In the event of a tie, the skater with the highest placement in the free skate wins. If two skaters are still tied, first place goes to the skater with the highest artistic marks in the free skate.

Glossary of Skating Terms

Axel: a difficult jump and the only one that takes off forward. The axel is landed backward, so a "single" involves rotating in the air one and a half times. Norway's Axel Paulsen created the jump in 1882.

Camel: a spin in which the skater leans forward, arches her back, and holds her free leg up behind her so that her body is in the shape of a T.

Choreography: the arrangement of movements, steps, and patterns in a program.

Clean: describes a jump that is landed without wobbles or falls.

Combination: several jumps performed one right after the other, so that the landing of the first jump becomes the takeoff for the next.

Death spiral: a dramatic movement in pairs skating in which the man holds his partner's hands and swings her around him in a circle. The woman's body is stretched out, and her head nearly touches the ice.

Edges: the two sharp sides of a skate blade, which border the slightly grooved center.

Flip jump: a jump that takes off with a push of the toe pick and lands on the opposite foot.

ISU: the International Skating Union.

Kiss and cry area: the nickname for the part of the rink where the skaters go to watch their scores come up.

Layback: a spin in which the skater leans her head and shoulders back.

Long program: the free skating portion of a competition, usually four minutes for women and four and a half minutes for men. This program counts for two thirds of a skater's final standing.

Loop jump: a jump that takes off from the back outside edge and lands on the same edge.

Lutz: a jump that takes off from the back outside edge and lands on the back outside edge of the other foot. German Alois Lutz created the jump in 1918.

Quad: short for quadruple. A jump with four revolutions in the air. So far, only men have landed quads in competitions, but women will probably start doing them soon.

Run-in: the "entrance" to a jump, during which a skater gains the speed she needs to leave the ice.

Salchow: a jump that takes off from a back inside edge and lands on the back outside edge of the other foot. The jump is named for its Swedish inventor, Ulrich Salchow.

School figures: shapes that skaters etched in the ice as part of competitions. The figures were judged on size and accuracy. This phase of competition was eliminated in 1990, mostly because figures aren't very interesting to watch.

Sit spin: a spin in which a skater starts in a standing position, then sinks down and extends one foot in front of her.

Spin: a move in which a skater turns in place like a top. A talented skater can complete as many as six rotations per second. While in a spin, a skater can speed up by pulling in her arms or slow down by extending them.

Spiral: a long glide in which the free leg is extended up and backward.

Technical program: a two-minute-and-forty-second performance set to music of the skater's choice, during which she must complete eight required elements in any sequence. Also called the short program. The performance counts as one third of a skater's final score.

Toe loop: a loop jump that takes off from the toe pick.

Toe pick: the ridged front section of the skate blade.

USFSA: the United States Figure Skating Association.

Waltz jump: an easy jump that resembles an axel but requires only half a rotation.

Zamboni: a large, lumbering machine that puts a new, smooth surface on the ice.